To Liz Sheard,
dear friend and excellent teacher.

With thanks to Pat Schaefer,
children's librarian and collector of fairy tales,
for her help and support.
And also to Megan Larkin and
Anna-Louise Billson, editor and designer.

ORCHARD BOOKS
Carmelite House
50 Victoria Embankment
London EC4Y 0DZ

First published in Great Britain in 1999
This edition first published in 2015
Text and Illustration © Helen Craig 1999
The right of Helen Craig to be identified as the author
and illustrator of this book has been asserted by her in accordance
with the Copyright, Designs and Patents Act, 1988.

A CIP catalogue for this book is available from the British Library.

ISBN: 978 1 40833 840 7
1 3 5 7 9 10 8 6 4 2
Printed in China

Orchard Books
An imprint of Hachette Children's Group
Part of The Watts Publishing Group Limited
An Hachette UK Company
www.hachette.co.uk

The Orchard Book of

Bedtime
Fairy Tales

HELEN CRAIG

ORCHARD

Contents

Contents

Little Red Riding Hood

Once upon a time there lived a girl called Little Red Riding Hood whose granny had made her a red cloak with a hood to keep her warm when she went out.

Granny, who lived in a cottage on the far side of the forest, was ill, and Little Red Riding Hood was taking her some cakes.

"Keep to the path and don't talk to strangers," called her mother.

"I promise," said Little Red Riding Hood.

She skipped through the forest. The sun shone and the birds sang. Little Red Riding Hood was happy.

But soon the sunlight got weaker and the forest grew quieter. Every now and then Little Red Riding Hood heard a strange sound.

Swish-swish. Swish-swish. Little Red Riding Hood drew her cloak tight around her.

As she went on, the forest grew even darker and the trees grew bigger. Little Red Riding Hood felt very small. *Swish-swish. Swish-swish.* Little Red Riding Hood walked faster.

Suddenly she came to a clearing full of flowers. "Oh! I'll pick some for Granny," she said, forgetting her fear and her mother's warning. She darted from flower to flower until she had a big bunch. But when she looked up, she couldn't see the path any more.

She began to cry.

"Can I help?" asked a voice behind her. Little Red Riding Hood turned and saw a wolf with a big bushy tail that went *swish-swish*. *Swish-swish*.

"Oh yes, please," sobbed Little Red Riding Hood. "I'm taking these cakes to my granny who is ill. She lives in the little cottage on the other side of the forest, but now I'm lost."

"I know the cottage. I can show you the way," said the wolf, careful not to show his sharp teeth.

He took Little Red Riding Hood to a path.

"This is the way to your granny's house," he said and he disappeared into the forest. *Swish-swish*. *Swish-swish*.

Now, this path was
twice as long as the one
Little Red Riding Hood
had been on before.
While she was taking
the long, twisty way, the
wolf hurried along the
shorter path and got to
Granny's cottage first.

He knocked at the cottage door. The grandmother thought it was Little Red Riding Hood, and called out, "Lift the latch and come in, my dear."

When she saw the wolf she fainted. The wolf put her under the bed to eat later. Then he put on her spare nightdress and cap and got into the bed to wait for Little Red Riding Hood. Very soon she arrived at the cottage and knocked on the door.

"Lift the latch and come in, my dear," squeaked the wolf in a high voice.

Little Red Riding Hood opened the door and came in. She looked hard at her granny.

"Oh, Granny, what big ears you have!" said Little Red Riding Hood.

"All the better to hear you with, my dear," croaked the wolf.

"Oh, Granny, what big eyes you have!" said Little Red Riding Hood.

"All the better to see you with, my dear," grinned the wolf.

"But Granny, what terrible big teeth you have!" said Little Red Riding Hood.

"All the better to eat you with," growled the wolf, and he leapt out of the bed and tried to catch Little Red Riding Hood.

But she was too quick for him and ran out of the door. Round and round the cottage the wolf chased after her.

A woodcutter working nearby saw the wolf chasing Little Red Riding Hood and he ran over and knocked the wolf down with his axe.

All the noise had woken up Granny and she came out from under the bed. She hugged Little Red Riding Hood and Little Red Riding Hood hugged the woodcutter and then they all sat down to enjoy the cakes that Little Red Riding Hood had brought in her basket.

The Gingerbread Man

Once upon a time a farmer's wife was baking
gingerbread for her husband. There was a little
bit left over and she decided to make a Gingerbread Man.
She gave him a head with currants for his eyes, his nose
and his mouth, and she gave him a body with arms and
legs. Then she put him in the oven to bake.

"Something smells nice," said the farmer when he
came home.

At that moment a little voice came from the oven.
"Open the door and let me out!" it said.

As soon as the farmer's wife opened the oven door,
the little Gingerbread Man jumped out. He ran out
of the kitchen door and into the farmyard, crying:

> "Run, run, run as fast as you can,
> You can't catch me, I'm the Gingerbread Man."

The farmer and his wife rushed out after the Gingerbread Man but they could not catch him.

He ran right past the farmer's dog.

"Hey stop," the dog woofed. "You look good to eat."

But the Gingerbread Man ran faster and as he ran he sang:

> "Run, run, run as fast as you can,
> You can't catch me, I'm the Gingerbread Man."

And the dog could not catch him.

The Gingerbread Man ran past the chickens in the yard.

"Hey stop," they clucked. "You would make some fine crumbs to eat."

But the Gingerbread Man ran faster, and as he ran he sang:

> "Run, run, run as fast as you can,
> You can't catch me, I'm the Gingerbread Man."

And the chickens could not catch him.

The Gingerbread Man ran past a cow in the field.

"Hey stop," she mooed. "You would make a tasty meal."

But the Gingerbread Man ran faster, and as he ran he sang:

"Run, run, run as fast as you can,
You can't catch me, I'm the Gingerbread Man."

And the cow could not catch him.

Then he met a fox. "Well, well, why are you running, my friend?" asked the fox.

"Oh," said the Gingerbread Man proudly, "I'm running from the farmer and his wife, and the dog and the chickens and the cow, and none of them can catch me." And he sang his song:

"Run, run, run as fast as you can,
You can't catch me, I'm the Gingerbread Man."

But the clever fox didn't try to catch him. He just followed quietly behind while the Gingerbread Man ran on. When they came to the river the Gingerbread Man stopped.

"How can I get across?" he said.

"I can help you," said the clever fox. "Climb onto my tail and I will take you across."

So the Gingerbread Man climbed onto the fox's tail and the fox started to swim across the river.

When they had gone a little way the fox said, "You are too heavy for my tail, little Gingerbread Man. Could you climb onto my back?"

So the Gingerbread Man climbed onto the fox's back. A little further on the fox said, "You are too heavy for my back, little Gingerbread Man. Could you climb onto my nose?"

So the Gingerbread Man climbed onto the fox's nose.

At last they reached the other side of the river.
The Gingerbread Man was about to jump down
from the fox's nose, when…

the fox opened his jaws wide and snapped him up – yum, yum – and that was the end of the Gingerbread Man.

The Three Little Pigs

There were once three little pigs and each little pig wanted to build himself a house. The first little pig collected some bundles of straw. "These will make a fine house," he said.

When he had finished, his straw house did look fine, and he moved in. He had just made himself a nice cup of tea when he heard the voice of the big bad wolf outside.

"Little pig, little pig, can I come in?" called the wolf in his sweetest voice.

"No, you cannot, not by the hair of my chinny-chin-chin," cried the little pig.

"Then I'll huff and I'll puff and I'll blow your house in," growled the wolf.

"Just you try," said the little pig, thinking he was good and safe in his fine straw house.

So the wolf huffed and he puffed and he blew that little straw house in.

"Oh, help! Help!" cried the little pig, and he ran all the way back to his mother.

"You got it all wrong," said the second pig to his brother. "I shall build *my* house of brushwood and you can come and live with me."

So the second pig collected a great heap of brushwood. "This will make me a fine house," he said.

When he had finished, his brushwood house did look fine, and he moved in. He was just settling down to a large slice of apple tart when he heard the big bad wolf outside.

"Little pig, little pig, can I come in?" called the wolf in his sweetest voice.

"No, you cannot, not by the hair of my chinny-chin-chin," said the second little pig.

"Then I'll huff and I'll puff and I'll blow your house in," growled the wolf.

"You just try," said the little pig, thinking his brushwood house was strong and safe.

So the wolf huffed and he puffed and he blew that little brushwood house in.

"Oh help! Help!" cried the second little pig, and he ran right back to his mother.

The third little pig didn't say anything, but he had been watching all the time and he had a plan.

He went to the brickyard and bought a big load of bricks
and some bags of cement, strong windows and an even stronger
door, and then he built his house with a fireplace and a fine
chimney. The wolf watched from his hiding place and waited.

At last, when the third little pig had finished his house, he
invited his two brothers in to celebrate.

"Bring Mother's big cooking pot," he said, "and don't forget the lid."

The little pigs filled the cooking pot with water and set it on the fire to boil. Then they sat down to enjoy the plum cake their mother had sent them. Just then they heard the big bad wolf outside.

"Little pigs, little pigs, can I come in?" called the wolf in his sweetest voice.

"No, you cannot, not by the hair of my chinny-chin-chin," said the third little pig.

"Then I'll huff and I'll puff and I'll blow your house in," growled the wolf.

"Just you try," said the third little pig calmly.

The wolf huffed and he puffed but, try as he might, he could not blow that little brick house in.

So he tried the door, but it was strong and firmly bolted, and the window was locked too. Then he remembered the chimney.

"Aha – I'll get all three of them yet," he hissed.

The three little pigs heard the wolf scrambling up onto the roof.

But the third little pig was not worried.

He got the fire blazing well so that the water in the
pot began to bubble just as the wolf started to climb
down the chimney.

"Come and get us!" called the third little pig.

"I will, I will, just you wait," growled the wolf, but he was in such a hurry he missed his footing and fell headlong down the chimney and into the cooking pot.

The third little pig slapped on the lid and that was the end of the big bad wolf.

"What a mess," said the third little pig to his brothers. "Come on, let's clear up and then we can have tea."

So they did, and from then on the three little pigs all lived safely together in the little brick house.

The Magic Cooking Pot

Jenny lived alone with her mother. They were hungry because there was no money to buy food.

"I will go to look for berries in the forest," said Jenny, but she could not find any. She was wondering sadly what would become of her and her mother, when a little old woman came by.

"I have been watching you for a long time now, and I know what troubles you have," said the old woman. "So I have brought you a gift." From under her cloak she took out a little black cooking pot.

"Just put this pot on the fire and say, 'Boil, little pot' and it will make the most wonderful soup. When you have had enough, just say, 'Stop, little pot' and it will obey you."

Jenny thanked the old woman and raced home to her mother with the little black cooking pot. It worked! They had three bowls each of the most delicious tomato soup.

Now the little pot made a different soup every day and Jenny and her mother were never hungry.

One day Jenny had to go to market. At lunchtime, her mother wanted some soup.

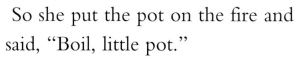

So she put the pot on the fire and said, "Boil, little pot."

Soon she was eating delicious vegetable soup.

Now she wanted it to stop, so she said, "Thank you, that will do." But the little pot continued to boil.

She said, "I have had my fill. Thank you."

The pot boiled on.

"That's enough!" she said crossly.

The little pot took no notice and went on cooking until the soup boiled over and covered the floor. Jenny's mother ran out of the house, and the soup, which was boiling faster and faster, followed.

It flowed down the hill and into the village. People climbed to the top rooms of their houses to escape the river of soup. Others got into boats and started to collect the soup in jugs and saucepans. Up the hill, in the cottage, the little pot was still boiling.

Just then Jenny, who was on her way home, met the soup oozing along the road. She knew immediately what had happened. She climbed up the nearest tree, took a deep breath and shouted as loud as she could:

"STOP, LITTLE POT!"

Up the hill, in the cottage, the little pot heard the order and stopped boiling.

The river of soup flowed out of the village, and past the forest. The animals did their best to drink it up and it took the villagers ages to clean their houses.

From now on Jenny took charge of the magic cooking pot and she and her mother were never hungry again. And they never had too much soup either.

The Little Red Hen

One sunny morning Little Red Hen was scratching about in her front garden, looking for seeds and worms to feed her chicks, when she came across some ears of wheat.

"There must be many grains of wheat here. We won't eat them now but I will plant them instead. Who will help me?" asked Little Red Hen.

"Not I," said the lazy dog, snoozing in the warm sun.

"Not I," said the cat, sleeping in the shadows.

"Not I," grunted the pig, lying on his bed of straw.

"Oh well, I will have to do it myself," said Little Red Hen, and she set to work.

She dug the ground and raked it. She sowed the grains of wheat and gave them some water. Then she waited.

Soon the grains had grown into tall stalks of ripe golden wheat.

"Now it is time to harvest the wheat," said Little Red Hen. "Who will help me cut it?"

"Not I," said the dog, rolling over and going to sleep again.

"Not I," said the cat, stretching and yawning.

"Not I," grunted the pig, opening one eye and shutting it again.

"Oh well then, I will have to do it myself," said Little Red Hen, and she set to work.

She cut the wheat with a sharp sickle and then she threshed it until she had a sack full of golden grain.

"Now the grain must go to the miller to be made into flour," said Little Red Hen. "Who will help me carry it?"

"Not I," said the dog as he flopped down in the grass.

"Not I," said the cat as she crept into her cosy corner.

"Not I," grumbled the pig as he trotted back to his sty.

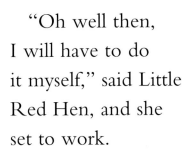

"Oh well then, I will have to do it myself," said Little Red Hen, and she set to work.

She hoisted the sack onto her back and trudged all the way to the miller.

The miller ground the golden grains of wheat between the large millstones and turned them into fine flour, which he put in a new clean sack and gave to Little Red Hen.

Little Red Hen carried the heavy sack of flour home.

"Now it is time to bake a cake," said Little Red Hen. "Who will help me?"

"Not I," said the lazy dog.

"Not I," said the sleepy cat.

"Not I," said the grumpy pig.

"Oh well then, I will have to do it myself," said Little Red
Hen, and she set to work.

She got milk and butter, and eggs and sugar, and some large
raisins and some small currants. She mixed them all together and
baked a most marvellous cake.

The good sweet smell drifted out over the garden.
"Now it is time to eat the cake. Who will help
me eat it?" asked Little Red Hen.

"I will," said the dog, wagging his tail.

"I will," said the cat, licking her lips.

"I will," said the pig, who couldn't wait.

"Oh no you won't!" said Little Red Hen. "You didn't help me plant the wheat or look after it. You didn't help me harvest it or take it to the miller. You didn't even help me bake the cake. So I will eat it all myself."

Which she did, with a little help from her chicks.

Goldilocks and the Three Bears

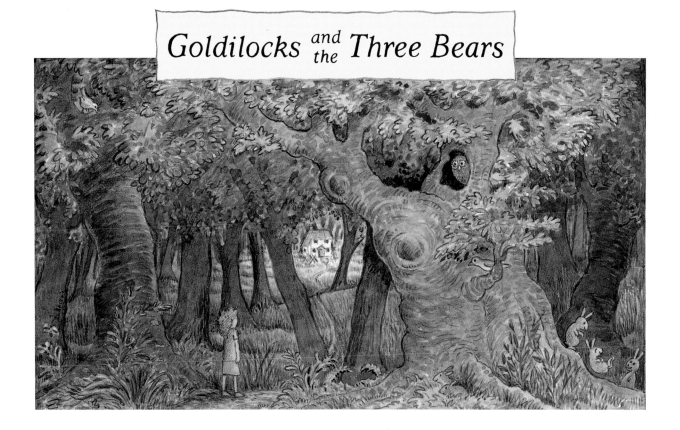

O nce upon a time there was a little girl called Goldilocks who lived with her father and mother on the edge of the forest.

"When can I go into the forest?" she kept asking. Her parents always replied, "You are too little. One day, when you are older, we will take you there."

But Goldilocks couldn't wait and, when nobody was looking, she slipped away into the forest. At first she enjoyed running in and out of the trees, but very soon she realised that she was lost.

She was frightened that she would never find her way back home. Then, through the trees, she saw a little house.

"Oh good! Now I can get some help," she thought.

The little house belonged to three bears. One was a Great Big Bear, one was a Middle-Sized Bear and one was a Small Baby Bear. They loved their little house and they kept it neat and tidy.

The Great Big Bear had just made a large pot of steaming hot porridge, which he poured into their bowls.

"The porridge is too hot to eat right now," he said in his big voice. "Let's go for a walk while it cools."

As the three bears left for their walk, Goldilocks arrived on the other side of the clearing.

She went up to the little house and rang the bell. There was no answer. She tapped on the window. There was no reply. So she gave the door a little push. It opened and she went in.

The porridge in the bowls smelled delicious. "I'm so hungry," said Goldilocks. "But I'll only take a little bit."

First she tried a spoonful from the Big Bear's large bowl, but it was too hot.

Next she tried a spoonful from the Middle Bear's medium-sized bowl, but it was too cold.

Then she tried a spoonful from the Baby Bear's little bowl. It was just right, and because she was so hungry she ate it all up!

Goldilocks was tired.

First she sat in the Big Bear's huge armchair, but it was too soft.

Next she sat in the Middle Bear's medium-sized chair, but it was too hard.

Then she sat in the
Baby Bear's little rocking
chair. It was just right.
She rocked backwards
and forwards until –
CRASH! – the bottom
of the chair broke.

Goldilocks went upstairs to the bears' neat little bedroom.
First she tried the Big Bear's enormous bed, but the pillows were too high.

Next she tried the Middle Bear's medium-sized bed, but the pillow was too low.

Finally she tried the Baby Bear's little bed. It was perfect and she fell fast asleep.

She was so fast asleep that she did not hear the three bears come home. The Great Big Bear sniffed the air. "Someone has been here," he said.

They saw the spoons in the bowls of porridge.

"Who's been eating my porridge?" said the Great Big Bear.

"Who's been eating my porridge?" said the Middle-Sized Bear.

"And who's been eating my porridge and eaten it all up!" cried the Small Baby Bear.

Then the Three Bears saw that the cushions in the armchairs were out of place.

"Who's been sitting in my chair?" rumbled the Great Big Bear.

"Who's been sitting in my chair?" grumbled the Middle-Sized Bear.

"And who's been sitting in my chair and BROKEN it!" squeaked the Small Baby Bear.

They ran upstairs and saw the rumpled beds.

"Who's been sleeping in MY bed?" roared the Great Big
Bear. Goldilocks slept on, dreaming of thunderstorms.

"Who's been sleeping in MY bed?" growled the Middle-Sized
Bear. Goldilocks dreamed a fierce wind was blowing.

"Look who's been sleeping in MY bed and is still there!" squealed the Small Baby Bear. His voice was so high and piercing that Goldilocks woke up with a start.

She was so frightened that she leapt from the bed, jumped out of the window and slid down the porch roof to the ground below.

She ran and she ran and she didn't stop running until she heard voices calling her name. It was her father and mother, and they were so pleased to see Goldilocks that they forgot to be cross with her for going into the forest alone. And Goldilocks was so happy to see them that she promised never to go off on her own again.

Lazy Jack

A long time ago there was a boy named Jack who lived with his mother. They were very, very poor. Jack's mother earned a little money spinning wool, but Jack was a lazy boy. In the summer he lay in the sun, and in the winter he lounged by the fire. He never did any work.

At last his mother got cross. "Lazy Jack," she said, "it's time you did some work and earned some money. Or else it's time you left home."

Well, Jack was happy at home and did not want to leave, so the next day he went out to look for a job. He found work with a farmer who paid him one penny at the end of the day. But on his way home Jack lost the penny.

"You stupid boy!" said his mother. "You should have put it in your pocket."

"I'll remember for next time," said Jack.

The next day, Jack worked for a farmer who paid him with a jug of milk. Jack put the jug in his pocket. But by the time he got home, all the milk had spilled out and messed up his clothes.

"You stupid boy!" said his mother. "You should have carried it on your head."

"I'll remember for next time," said Jack.

The day after, Jack worked for another farmer who gave him a big creamy cheese.

Jack remembered what his mother had said, and put the cheese on his head. But by the time he got home, the cheese had dribbled down his face and was stuck in his hair.

"You stupid boy!" said his mother. "You should have carried it in your hands."

"I'll remember for next time," said Jack.

The next day, Jack
worked for a baker who
gave him a large tom-cat for
his wages. So Jack took care
to carry the cat in
his hands.

But the cat fought
and scratched so
hard that Jack had
to let him go.

"You stupid boy!" said
his mother. "You should
have tied it with a piece of
string and pulled it along
after you."

"I'll remember for next
time," said Jack.

The following day, Jack went to work for a butcher who gave him a large leg of mutton. Jack tied a piece of string to the mutton and dragged it along after him. But by the time he got home the leg of mutton was so dirty that it was no good to eat any more.

His mother was very upset. They could have had a nice roast, but now they would have to eat boiled cabbage again.

"You really are a stupid boy!" she cried. "You should have carried it on your shoulders."

"I'll remember for next time," said Jack.

On the following Monday, Jack worked for a cattle dealer at the market who gave him a donkey for his hard day's work. Jack was determined to do it right this time. He heaved and heaved until at last he managed to lift the donkey onto his shoulders, and, holding it by the head and tail, he set off home.

Now, on his way, Jack had to pass the house of a very rich man and his beautiful daughter. The daughter was deaf and mute and very sad. The doctors said she would never hear or speak until someone made her laugh.

People had tried all sorts of tricks, but nothing worked. Finally, her father promised that the first man who could make her laugh would marry her and inherit all his riches.

Now, the daughter happened to see Jack passing by with the donkey on his shoulders. The sight was so funny that she just couldn't help it – she burst out laughing. Her father was overjoyed. He rushed out and invited Jack in for tea.

When Jack put down the donkey, it ran off. But it didn't matter that he had lost his day's wages again, because Jack and the girl fell in love and married and Jack became a rich man. They lived in a grand house and Jack's mother came to live with them, and she never called Jack stupid or lazy again.

The Three Billygoats Gruff

O nce upon a time there were three Billygoats Gruff. There was Big Billygoat Gruff, Middle Billygoat Gruff and Little Billygoat Gruff.

The three billygoats had eaten all the grass on the hill where they lived and they were hungry. Over the river they could see another hill of rich green grass and they longed to go and eat there. But the river was deep and dangerous and the only bridge was guarded by a fierce and terrible troll. Nobody ever got across the bridge because he ate everyone who tried.

The three Billygoats Gruff felt hungrier and hungrier as they stared at the lovely green grass.

Finally, Little Billygoat Gruff could bear it no longer.

He set off to cross the bridge. TRIP-TRAP, TRIP-TRAP went his hooves on the wooden bridge. He was halfway across when the fierce and terrible troll stepped out and barred his way.

"Who dares to cross my bridge?" roared the troll.

"It's only me, Little Billygoat Gruff," said Little Billygoat Gruff. "I'm going to eat the green grass on the other side."

"Oh, no you're not," growled the troll, "because I am going to eat *you* first!"

"Oh, please, you don't want to bother eating me," said Little Billygoat Gruff. "I am so small. But if you wait a while my older brother will be along. He is bigger and fatter than me and will make a much better meal."

"That sounds like a good idea," said the troll, and he let Little Billygoat Gruff pass over. "After all," he chuckled to himself, "I can always eat the little one when he returns and that way I will have two meals."

After a while, Middle Billygoat Gruff came along. TRIT-TROT, TRIT-TROT went his hooves on the wooden bridge. He was halfway across when the fierce and terrible troll jumped out and barred his way.

"Who dares to cross my bridge?" roared the troll.

"It's only me, Middle Billygoat Gruff," said Middle Billygoat Gruff. "I am going to eat the grass on the other side."

"Oh, no you're not," growled the troll, "because I am going to eat *you* first!"

"Oh, please, you don't want to bother eating me," said Middle Billygoat Gruff. "I'm all skin and bones. If you wait a little longer my older brother will be along. He is bigger and fatter than me and will make a much better meal!"

"That sounds like a good idea," said the troll and he let Middle Billygoat Gruff pass over.

"After all," chuckled the greedy troll, "I can always eat the middle one, too, when he returns, and that way I can have three meals!"

Then Big Billygoat Gruff came along. **TRAMP-TRAMP**, **TRAMP-TRAMP** went his hooves on the wooden bridge. He was halfway across when the fierce and terrible troll leapt out and barred his way.

"Who dares to cross my bridge?" roared the troll.

"It's me, Big Billygoat Gruff," said Big Billygoat Gruff, "and I'm going to eat the grass on the other side."

"Oh, no you're not," roared the troll, "because I am going to eat *you* first!"

"Oh, you are, are you?"
shouted Big Billygoat Gruff,
and he put his head down
and charged.

The troll let out a terrible
yell and rushed at Big
Billygoat Gruff.

But Big Billygoat Gruff was
brave and he didn't stop.
He caught the troll on his
horns and tossed him right
over the bridge.

Down,
        down
            into the deep river
fell the troll, and he was
never seen again.

Big Billygoat Gruff passed over the bridge and joined his brothers on the grassy hill. They ate as much as they wanted, and when they came home that evening there was no one to stop them.

Chicken Licken

One morning, Chicken Licken was in the wood, when an acorn fell on his head.

"Oh, my goodness! The sky is falling!" cried Chicken Licken. "I must go and tell the King." So Chicken Licken set off. On the way he met Henny Penny.

"Hello, Chicken Licken, where are you going?" she asked.

"Oh Henny Penny, the sky is falling!" cried Chicken Licken. "This morning I was in the wood when the sky fell on my head and so I am going to tell the King."

"How terrible!" exclaimed Henny Penny. "I will come too." And they set off together.

On the way they met Cocky Locky.

"Hello you two, where are you off to?" he asked.

"Oh Cocky Locky, the sky is falling!" said Henny Penny.
"I met Chicken Licken who was in the wood this morning
when the sky fell on his head, so we are going to tell
the King."

"How dreadful!" exclaimed Cocky Locky. "I will come too."
And they set off together.

After a while they met Ducky Lucky.

"Hello you three, where are you going?" she asked.

"Oh Ducky Lucky, the sky is falling!" said Cocky Locky. "I met Henny Penny who met Chicken Licken. He was in the wood this morning when the sky fell on his head, so we are going to tell the King."

"Oh dear, oh dear!" exclaimed Ducky Lucky. "I will come too." And they set off together.

A little further on they met Drakey Lakey.

"Hello you four, where are you off to?" he asked.

"Oh, Drakey Lakey, the sky is falling!" said Ducky Lucky. "I met Cocky Locky who met Henny Penny who met Chicken Licken. He was down in the wood this morning when the sky fell on his head, so we are going to tell the King."

"How awful!" exclaimed Drakey Lakey. "I will come too." And they set off together.

Along the way they met Goosey Loosey.

"Hello you five, where are you going?" she asked.

"Oh Goosey Loosey, the sky is falling!" said Drakey Lakey. "I met Ducky Lucky who met Cocky Locky who met Henny Penny who met Chicken Licken. He was in the wood this morning when the sky fell on his head, so we are going to tell the King."

"This is bad news!" exclaimed Goosey Loosey. "I will come too." And they set off together.

They hadn't gone far when they met Turkey Lurkey.

"Hello you six, where are you off to?" he asked.

"Oh Turkey Lurkey, the sky is falling!" said Goosey Loosey. "I met Drakey Lakey who met Ducky Lucky who met Cocky Locky who met Henny Penny who met Chicken Licken. He was in the wood this morning when the sky fell on his head, so we are going to tell the King."

"This is very serious!" exclaimed Turkey Lurkey. "I will come too." And they set off together.

A little way down the road they met Foxy Loxy.

"Hello my seven friends, where are you off to?" he asked. So they told Foxy Loxy that the sky had fallen on Chicken Licken's head and they were going to tell the King.

"Do you know where the King lives?" asked Foxy Loxy.
"No we don't, can you tell us please?" they replied.
"Certainly I can, just follow me," said the fox.

But Foxy Loxy took them straight to his den where Mrs Foxy Loxy and all the little Foxy Loxys were waiting for their dinner.

The foxes ate up poor Chicken Licken, Henny Penny, Cocky Locky, Ducky Lucky, Drakey Lakey, Goosey Loosey and Turkey Lurkey. So they never did tell the King that the sky was falling down.

The Shoemaker *and the* Elves

Long ago there lived an honest shoemaker and his wife. Although they worked hard, they never had enough money and they grew poorer and poorer.

The day came when the shoemaker had only enough leather to make one more pair of shoes. That evening, as he always did, he cut out the leather pieces and laid them on the workbench ready for the next day. Then he went to bed.

Early next morning he went to his bench to start work, but there, to his amazement, stood a finished pair of shoes.

They were perfect – not a stitch missing, not a stitch wrong.

Who had done the work?

Later on a customer came to the little shop. The shoes pleased him so much that he happily paid double the usual price for them. With the money, the shoemaker was able to buy enough leather to make two pairs of shoes.

That evening he cut the pieces of leather and laid them out ready for the next day. When he got up in the morning, once again the work was done! There on the bench were two pairs of perfect shoes – not a stitch missing, not a stitch wrong.

Two customers came that morning and paid a good price for the perfect shoes. Now the shoemaker was able to buy enough leather for four pairs of shoes. He cut out the leather that night and in the morning, as before, the shoes were ready, and the shoemaker sold all four pairs for a good price.

This went on for many months, and the shoemaker and his wife grew rich and prosperous.

Just before Christmas they were sitting by the fire, talking.

"I would like to stay up tonight," said the shoemaker, "and see who is doing the work that helps us so much."

His wife agreed, and so they left a candle burning on the workbench, hid themselves behind a curtain, and waited.

On the stroke of midnight two tiny elves crept through a gap in the door. Despite the cold snow outside, the elves wore not a stitch of clothing!

They climbed onto the shoemaker's bench and started to
work. They stitched and hammered and hammered and stitched
at such a speed that the shoemaker and his wife were spellbound.

Soon they were finished. There on the bench stood a whole row of perfect shoes. Not a stitch missing, not a stitch wrong! The elves jumped down and vanished through the gap in the door.

The next morning the shoemaker's wife said, "Those little people have made us rich and comfortable. We ought to do something for them in return. The poor little things have no clothes to keep them warm. I will make them each a little shirt and a coat, a waistcoat and a pair of trousers, and you can make them each a pair of little boots."

The idea pleased the shoemaker. He went to choose the softest leather for the little boots while his wife searched in her workbasket for the brightest pieces of cloth she could find.

Then they set to work, stitching and sewing.

At last, on Christmas Eve, the clothes were ready.
The shoemaker and his wife laid out each garment on the
workbench instead of the pieces of leather.

Then they hid themselves behind the curtain again,
and waited.